CONTENTS

MINA (the Vampire)

Mina thinks people taste like dirty socks, so beetroot juice is her snack of choice. Its red colour has fooled her parents into thinking that she's a traditional blood-sucking vampire instead of a superhero. She has the ability to change into a bat or a mouse at will.

Brian is the brainy one amongst his friends. Unlike other zombies, Brian prefers tofu to brains. No matter what sort of trouble is brewing, Brian always comes up with a plan to save the day, like a true superhero.

BRIAN (the Zombie)

WILL (the Ghost)

Will is quite shy. Luckily he can become invisible whenever he wants to, because he is a ghost. When Will is doing good deeds, he likes to remain unseen. His invisibility helps him to be brave like a real superhero.

With a wave of her wand and a poetic chant, Linda can reverse any magical curse. She hopes to use her magic to help people, just like a superhero would.

LINDA (the Witch)

FAMILY HOLIDAY

Mina felt a chill. Lights in the train flashed. People gasped in fear. But Mina's friend Linda, the witch, was not afraid.

Mina's parents sat in the seats opposite her and Linda. They were all going to visit Mina's great-great-great-grandpa Drac. It was his birthday.

"That is so cool!" Linda said. "Look!"

Outside, the landscape quickly changed. The sunny blue sky turned dark and gloomy. Bare, creepy trees replaced the leafy, bright trees.

A moment ago, sheep had been baaing. *BAA! BAA!*

Now, wolves growled. *GRR! GRR!*

"We are now entering Transylvania!" the train conductor announced.

Transylvania was the scariest place on Earth. It was even scarier than Mrs Johnson's maths lessons!

"This is going to be so much fun," Linda said.

Mina sighed.

Linda knew Mina was nervous about meeting her great-great-great-grandpa. He was a traditional vampire. He liked to suck people's blood.

Mina did not suck blood. She drank beetroot juice instead. Only her best friends knew her secret.

The train chugged along. The scenery grew darker. Mina continued to worry about meeting her grandpa.

"Next stop, Bran Castle," the conductor announced.

The train stopped.

SCRRREEEEEECH!

Mina, Linda and Mina's parents grabbed their bags and headed for the door.

GRANDPA DRAC

A small vampire waited outside for them. "Hey, cousin!" he shouted.

"Mina, this is your cousin, Spike," Mina's dad said. "He's your age."

Spike beamed a toothy grin. Mina smiled with her mouth closed.

"Whoa! You have sharp fangs," Linda said.

"All the better to bite with," Spike replied. Mina's parents laughed.

"He's such a sweetie," Mina's mum said.

"Come on! Let me show you girls the castle," Spike said.

He dragged Mina and Linda up the many steps leading to the castle. The doors creaked open. A dark figure stood before them.

"Hey, Gramps!" Spike said.

"Happy birthday, Grandpa Drac!" Mina said.

"Grumble, grumble," Grandpa Drac said.

"What did he say?" Linda whispered in Mina's ear.

Mina shrugged.

"Oops, I forgot I had these with me," Spike said.

He pulled some false teeth from his pocket and gave them to Grandpa Drac.

"I said," Grandpa Drac repeated, "we are having tourists for dinner."

He pointed to a group of people walking up the stairs.

"And there are 1,431 steps to the front door," the tour guide was saying.

The tourists replied "Ooh", "Ah" and "Where is the lift?"

Mina knew that people often came to see her grandfather's creepy old castle. But they didn't often leave.

"Oh no," Mina gasped.

"Those tourists aren't here for dinner. They ARE dinner!" Linda said.

Spike saw that the girls were worried. So he said, "Come on! Let me show you my room."

Spike led Mina and Linda up to his room.

"I'm not like other vampires," Spike said. "I don't like the taste of people."

"I don't either!" Mina said. "They taste like dirty socks."

"Yeah, soaked in pickle juice," Spike added.

"So you don't suck blood either?" Linda asked.

"Nope," Spike said. "I only bite beetroot."

"Me too," Mina said with a smile.

"That gives me an idea," Linda said as she pulled out her wand.

A NEW RECIPE

Mina, Linda and Spike sneaked down to the kitchen. Unfortunately, Mina's mum and dad were also in the kitchen.

"Are you here to help with dinner?" Mina's dad asked.

"No, no," Spike said. "We are here to *make* dinner."

"We want to make something extra special for Grandpa Drac," Mina said.

Once Mina's parents were out of the kitchen, the three monsters got to work.

"I'll get the beetroot," Mina said.

"I'll do the cooking," Linda said.

"And I'll help the tourists to escape," Spike said.

First, Spike led the tourists out of the back door. Then, Mina dropped the beetroot into a black pot. Linda waved her wand and chanted.

"Hippity, hoppity, hippity-boo. I'm gonna make us beetroot stew."

POOF!

The kids called the adults in to dinner. They served beetroot stew and beetroot juice.

"This tastes odd," Grandpa Drac said.

"It definitely tastes different," Mina's dad said.

Mina, Linda and Spike froze. The adults were going to work out the big secret!

"But it certainly is delicious!" Mina's mum said.

"It sure is," Mina's dad said. "What recipe did you use?"

"An old classic that can't be beaten," Spike said, smiling.

Linda and Mina couldn't help but laugh.

"Cheers!" Spike said.

"Cheers!" everyone replied.

DAVE BARDIN

Dave Bardin studied illustration while working as an art teacher. As an artist, Dave has worked on many different projects for television, books, comics and animation. In his spare time Dave enjoys watching documentaries, listening to podcasts, travelling and spending time with friends and family.

BLAKE HOENA

Blake Hoena grew up in Wisconsin, USA, where he wrote stories about robots conquering the Moon and trolls lumbering around the woods behind his house. He now lives in Minnesota, USA, and continues to write about fun things such as space aliens and superheroes. Blake has written more than fifty chapter books and graphic novels for children.

GLOSSARY

beetroot vegetable with thick leaves and a rounded red root

fang long, pointed tooth

gasp breathe in quickly

gloomy somewhat dark and sad

scenery natural parts of a landscape, such as trees, lakes and mountains

tourist person who travels to different places for fun or adventure

THINK ABOUT IT

1. Mina is nervous about meeting her grandfather. Have you ever been nervous about meeting someone new? What did you do to make yourself feel more comfortable?

2. Do you think Mina and Spike did the right thing by letting the tourists go and not telling their parents? Why or why not?

3. Mina and Spike are cousins, but they had never met before her visit to the castle. Talk about a family member you love to spend time with.

WRITE ABOUT IT

1. Mina and Spike tell their family that the beetroot stew is "an old classic that can't be beaten". Make a list of foods that your family makes when they celebrate something or spend time together.

2. Imagine you are going to visit Bran Castle. Make a list of things to pack. What would you take with you?

3. Linda, Mina and Mina's family are all going to visit Grandpa Drac for his birthday. What is the most memorable birthday you've had? Write a few sentences describing it.

THE FUN DOESN"T STOP HERE!

Discover more at
www.raintree.co.uk